GREAT ILLUSTRATED CLASSICS

FRANKENSTEIN

Mary Shelley

adapted by
Malvina G. Vogel

Illustrations by
Pablo Marcos Studio

**BARONET
BOOKS**

BARONET BOOKS, New York, New York

Contents

CHAPTER   PAGE

1. Rescued from the Frozen Sea 7
2. The Frankenstein Story Begins 21
3. Discovering an Astonishing Secret 29
4. Creating the Monster 39
5. The Spark of Life 45
6. Madness! 51
7. The First Murder! 65
8. Sighting the Monster 73
9. A Sad Homecoming 81
10. Justine Moritz—the Second Victim 87
11. Face to Face with the Monster 97
12. The Monster's Story Begins 107
13. A Confession of Murder 129
14. A Terrible Promise 139
15. Beginning a Second Creature 147
16. The Monster's Threat 159
17. The Murderer Strikes Again! 169
18. Imprisoned for Murder! 185
19. A Joyous Wedding 195
20. A Wedding Night Victim! 203
21. A Worldwide Search Begins 211
22. Peace At Last! 225

About the Author

It is not surprising that Mary Shelley became a writer, since her parents were famous writers in 18th-century England. What *is* surprising, however, is that when Mary was barely nineteen, her imagination created one of the greatest horror stories of all time.

As a child, Mary loved to read and to "scribble"—her description of her favorite pastime of writing stories. Her childhood was spent in the company of many famous writers and poets, who were her father's friends. Among these poets was Percy Bysshe Shelley, who later became Mary's husband.

Percy Shelley encouraged his wife to write, but Mary was happy being a wife and mother, and traveling with her husband. She gave little thought to writing until the summer of 1816, when the Shelleys were on a vacation at a lakeside villa in Switzerland.

The weather at Lake Geneva had turned cold and rainy, and Mary and Percy spent many days and nights in front of the fire with their very good friend, the poet Lord Byron.

To pass the time, the group began reading ghost stories to each other, then decided to make up their own. The men made up their stories easily, but Mary spent days trying to make up one that would be as exciting and horrifying as those they had been reading.

One night, Mary lay awake thinking about a discussion the men had had earlier that evening about the possibility of a corpse being "reanimated" and "a creature manufactured." When she finally fell asleep, Mary's dreams were filled with a story of just such a creature. She told the story to Percy and Lord Byron the following day—the day that *Frankenstein* was born.

Since its publication 175 years ago, this immortal horror story, from the pen of a nineteen-year-old girl, has been fascinating millions of readers and movie audiences, in hundreds of languages, all over the world!

The Threatening Arctic Ice

CHAPTER 1

Rescued from the Frozen Sea

The floating sheets of Arctic ice were slowly freezing together, threatening to crush the small sailing ship.

Robert Walton, its young English captain, stood on deck, wondering if he were wrong risking the lives of his brave crew for his own ambitions—to explore oceans ships had never sailed on and land men had never walked on.

He dreamed of the benefits this discovery would have for all mankind if he were to discover a sea route near the North Pole from Europe to Asia.

Walton had been born into wealth and could have chosen to spend his life in ease and luxury. Instead, he had spent the last six years at sea, working as a common sailor, enduring cold, hunger, thirst, sleeplessness, and often brutal discipline, just to prepare his body and mind for this long and dangerous voyage.

But now, with the ice threatening his ship and the lives of his crew, it was doubtful whether or not any of them would ever see their homes and families in England again!

At about two o'clock in the afternoon, the thick, heavy fog that had surrounded the ship all morning began to lift. As it did, a strange sight appeared on the ice.

"Look, Captain!" called a crewman, pointing to a dark spot a half-mile away. "It's a sledge, sir. And those dogs are pulling it as if their feet had wings!"

Walton lifted his telescope to his eye. "And look at that driver!" he cried. "He has to be

Sighting a Sledge

the most gigantic man I've ever laid eyes on! What on earth is he doing here, out in the middle of the frozen sea, hundreds of miles away from any land?"

Within minutes, though, the mysterious traveler had disappeared on the ice, leaving Walton and his crew stunned and speechless!

The next morning at dawn, Walton came up on deck to find his sailors leaning over the rail, apparently talking to someone on the ice below.

"What's happening, lads?" he asked as he joined them at the rail.

"It's a sledge, sir," said a sailor, "much like the one we saw yesterday."

Walton looked out over the rail. There, frozen into a block of ice drifting towards the ship was a sledge, a dog team, and a driver. All the dogs were dead except one, and its reins were being held limply by a frost-covered man as he paddled the block of ice with a piece of wood. He appeared to be barely alive.

A Surprising Discovery!

"This isn't the same sledge we saw yesterday," Walton told his men, "and this man is nothing at all like that gigantic creature that sped past us."

"Here is our captain," called one of the sailors to the man below. "Perhaps he can persuade you to come aboard."

"Good Lord, man! You're near death!" called Walton. "Let my men bring you up."

"Thank you, sir," answered the man in a weak voice, "but first I need to know where your ship is headed."

Walton was amazed that anyone so near death should ask such a question of anyone interested in saving his life. But he decided to humor the man by explaining, "We're exploring the seas near the North Pole."

The man nodded and whispered, "North is good." And he let the sailors come down to carry him up to the ship.

Once the man was on deck, the ship's doctor reported, "His legs are nearly frozen, sir,

Rescuing a Man Near Death

and his body is so thin that his bones are coming through his clothing."

"Wrap him in blankets and lay him gently near the stove," ordered Walton. "When he warms up, feed him a little soup, then put him in my cabin. He'll be comfortable there, and I will take care of him myself."

For two days, the man didn't speak. The wild expression in his eyes and the frequent gnashing of his teeth made Walton fear that the man's suffering had driven him mad. Yet there were moments, when someone was kind or helpful to him, that his eyes shone with kindness and gratitude.

When the man was finally able to utter a few words, Walton asked him, "What were you doing out there on the ice in a sledge?"

The man's face immediately turned gloomy as he replied, "I'm looking for someone in a sledge very much like mine."

"We saw him," Walton explained, "only the day before we picked you up."

Feeding the Starving Man

At that news, the stranger's eyes opened wide, and he raised himself off the pillow. "Which way did that demon head?" he gasped. "How many dogs did he have? How much food? I must know! I must find him!"

"Calm yourself, my friend," cautioned Walton. "You've been very ill, and you mustn't have this kind of excitement."

"You're right," said the stranger with a sigh. "You've rescued me from near death, and I'm certain that you must be curious about me. My grief is so deep that I can't talk about it yet, but please be patient. I have a terrible secret which I promise to share with you very soon."

Days passed, and the man's strength returned. He insisted on spending his time on deck searching for the sledge, but he also enjoyed hearing Captain Walton talk about his dreams of exploration.

"Yes, my friend," explained the young Englishman, "I would gladly sacrifice my fortune

A Promise to Share a Secret

and even my life to gain the knowledge that this voyage could bring. They would be a small price to pay for something that could benefit all mankind."

The stranger covered his eyes with his hands, and tears fell from beneath his fingers. "Don't talk that way! You'll be an unhappy man!" he cried. "As I tell you my story, you'll see how I devoted my life to seeking knowledge that I believed would benefit mankind. As a result, I brought misery and death to everyone I loved, and I'm now near death myself. Don't let that happen to you."

"Perhaps talking about your misfortune will help you," Walton said gently. "And perhaps I can do something to help also."

"I thank you for your sympathy," said the man, "but nothing can change my destiny. I have to do one more thing while I'm alive, then I'll be able to die in peace."

They went below and he began his story.

"Nothing Can Change My Destiny."

A Happy, Devoted Family

CHAPTER 2

The Frankenstein Story Begins

My name is Victor Frankenstein, and for generations my family has been one of the most respected in the government of Geneva, Switzerland. My devoted parents raised me and my two younger brothers, Ernest and William, with patience and love, and even brought into our family Elizabeth Lavenza, the orphaned daughter of a noble Italian family.

Elizabeth was a year younger than I, and I truly loved her as my sister, even though we called her my cousin. We spent many happy hours together as we grew up. Elizabeth loved the wonderful sights of nature in the mountains and lakes of Switzerland . . . while I was more interested in investigating *why* things in nature happened . . . what secrets the heavens and earth were hiding from me!

When I started school, I formed a lifelong friendship with Henry Clerval. Henry was a hard-working but spirited boy. He enjoyed writing adventure stories of heroic knights, then getting me to act them out with him.

What a happy childhood I had! Kind, generous parents, a loving sister, two happy, young brothers, and a devoted, fun-loving friend. All this . . . before my life was ruined . . . before my wild ambition drove me to unlocking the secrets of nature that had been hidden from man since life on Earth began.

But at the age of thirteen, my only interest in science was to discover a way to cure disease, to stop people from dying.

How noble were these childhood dreams!

Playing the Heroic Knights

When I was fifteen, a violent thunderstorm added to my scientific curiosity. A sudden, frightening burst of lightning struck an old oak tree near our house. In moments, the tree was gone, leaving only thin ribbons of wood in its place.

I had never before seen anything so completely demolished. At that moment, I suddenly realized what incredible but destructive powers electricity had. From then on, I began to wonder what other unknown powers electricity might be hiding from the world!

This curiosity was still with me when I was seventeen and preparing to leave home to study at the University of Ingolstadt, a small school in Germany.

Before I left, however, I was faced with the first misfortune of my life. Elizabeth had caught a serious case of scarlet fever, and her life was in great danger. Although we had servants to care for her, my mother insisted on caring for Elizabeth herself, in

The Power of Electricity!

spite of the fact that she was exposing herself to this terrible disease. Within three days, my mother came down with the fever, and by the fourth day, she was close to death.

As she lay dying, my mother called the family together and placed Elizabeth's hand in mine. "Take care of your brothers," she said. "I shall die happy if I know that one day you two will marry each other."

Elizabeth and I made that promise.

I didn't want to leave the family after my mother's death, but after several weeks, my father decided it was time.

Henry came to say goodbye. We were distressed at being separated. He was eager for a university education too, but his father wouldn't allow it, since he had plans for Henry to go to work in his business one day.

As I waved goodbye and climbed into the carriage, I realized that for the first time in my life, I was facing the world alone.

A Promise to a Dying Mother

Professor Waldman Encourages Victor.

CHAPTER 3

Discovering an Astonishing Secret

My boyhood dreams for studying science continued at the university. My aim was still to find ways to cure disease and prolong human life.

I was encouraged to study both modern and ancient scientists by Professor Waldman, my favorite teacher. "By combining knowledge from both," he told me, "you'll have unlimited powers. You'll be able to discover the secrets of the earth and the heavens, along with the secrets of man's body and how it works."

"But, sir," I protested, "I want to discover more than just the secrets of how the human body *works*." And it was at that moment that I knew I had to discover the secrets of how the human body was *created*!

Seeing my eyes glowing with enthusiasm, but not imagining where my ambition was heading, Professor Waldman promised me, "My boy, I'm delighted with your attitude and proud of your desire to succeed. You can be sure I'll give you all the help you need."

Professor Waldman became my friend as well as my teacher during the next two years. I read every scientific paper I could find, attended every lecture possible, and talked with the great scientists at the university.

I set up a laboratory on the top floor of my apartment house and worked most nights straight through until dawn.

Professor Waldman called me into his laboratory one morning. "Victor, your progress has been amazing these past two years."

At Work Through Most Nights

"Thank you, sir. I'm now devoting more time to the study of anatomy and physiology, so that one day I can discover how human life begins. But I know that to do that, I must first study how life ends—how the body dies and decays."

"That is a most ambitious project, Victor. Scientists have been trying to unlock those secrets since the world began. You are a brilliant scientist, destined for greatness. If anyone can do it, you can. But you must not ignore the world around you and the people who love you. . . . By the way, do you realize it's been two years since you went home to visit your family in Geneva?"

"My work is too important now for me to take time out for a visit," I told him.

And the professor didn't press me on it.

For the next months, I spent days and nights in charnel houses, the church buildings where corpses were kept until they were buried. I learned what happened to people's

Studying Corpses in Charnel Houses

bodies right after death, but I needed to know more—I needed to know how death changed the human body as weeks, months, and even years passed. To learn this, I secretly visited cemeteries on dark nights and dug up bodies to study them.

Months of studying and experimenting led to one memorable night when a wondrous light turned on in my brain. *In that one astonishing moment, I suddenly understood not only how life turned into death . . . but how death could be turned back into life!*

This realization made me so dizzy, all I could do was ask myself, "Why didn't the great scientists who came before me discover this secret? Why have *I* been blessed with unlocking the mysteries of creation?"

What followed next were weeks and months of incredible work and fatigue. Not only had I discovered the origin of life, but I continued experimenting until I was actually able to *create* life from lifeless matter!

Digging Up Long-Dead Bodies To Study

FRANKENSTEIN

The joy I felt made me forget the painful weeks and months I had spent on my work. All I knew was that I had discovered something that men of science had been trying to discover since the world began!

* * * * * *

At this point in Victor Frankenstein's story, Robert Walton interrupted. "Amazing!" he cried. "And are you about to share your secret with me, my friend?"

Victor shook his head sadly. "I can't, Robert. I know I owe you my life, and because of that, I ask you to please just listen to the rest of my story. Then you'll understand why I can't share my secret with you ... or anyone else on earth. For if you were to learn that terrible secret, you would be destroyed just as I have been!"

Overjoyed at His Amazing Discovery!

Wondering What To Put Life Into

CHAPTER 4

Creating the Monster

Why do I say that I've been destroyed? I say it because the knowledge and power that the secret gave me was more than I, or any man for that matter, could handle.

At first, I spent a great deal of time wondering how to use that knowledge. I knew how to create life, but what should I put that life into? I would need some sort of form in which to put muscles, bones, organs, arteries, veins, and other body parts.

Should I try to create a simple animal creature or a person like myself?

My wild imagination soared, and I truly believed I could do *anything* with this new knowledge. Yes, I would give life to a creature as complex and as wonderful as a human being!

Because of all the intricate parts that make up a human body, I decided that the creature couldn't be small or even of normal size. It would have to be gigantic, about eight feet tall, for me to be able to attach all the body parts, inside and outside.

I spent the next several months collecting all the materials I would need: bones from bodies in charnel houses, animal parts from slaughter houses where meat was prepared for market, live animals I trapped or bought, body parts and instruments from the dissecting room at the university, and, yes, whole bodies which I dug up from graveyards!

During these months—it was summer when I began—I refused to rest. Night after night, through fall, winter, spring, and into the next

Collecting the Materials for a Human Body

summer and fall, I worked in my laboratory. I forgot to eat. I barely slept. I gave no thought at all to my family, even though in every letter I received, my father told me how worried he was.

There were times that I hated what I was doing. Then at other times, I was eager and impatient to finish my creation.

It was almost winter when my work was nearing success. But what price was my body paying for that success? My brain was tortured with fever. I had become so nervous that the noise of a leaf falling off a tree startled me. I had been avoiding everyone at the university for many months because my wrecked body was too frightening even for me to look at in the mirror!

But I told myself, "This will all disappear once my work is done, and I'll be back to my old healthy self again soon."

How wrong I was!

Tortured, Nervous, and Impatient!

Bringing the Creature to Life

CHAPTER 5

The Spark of Life

It was a dreary night in November when my work was finally finished. The rain beating at the windows drowned out the clanking of my instruments as I gathered all but a few and put them away.

I looked down at the lifeless creature that lay on the table before me and knew I was ready to give him life. The candle that lit my laboratory was nearly burned out, but it gave me enough light to touch the creature with my instruments. That touch created the spark that brought him to life!

FRANKENSTEIN

Slowly, the dull yellow eyes of the creature opened. A hard, raspy breath lifted his huge chest at the same time that his gigantic arms and legs began to jerk with convulsive movements.

I stared hard at this creature I had spent two years forming. Once, I had considered this a beautiful piece of work—the result of my life's dream, but now it filled me with horror and disgust!

His yellow skin was stretched over bones and muscles, barely covering them. His long, black hair flowed down over the shriveled skin on his grotesque face and thick neck, and his pearly white teeth contrasted with the straight, black lips surrounding them.

What had I done? . . . I couldn't bear looking at the horrible creature another minute, and I rushed out of the laboratory and down to my apartment.

Throwing myself on my bed, still with my clothes on, I hoped that sleep would erase from

Filled with Horror and Disgust

my brain the ugly picture of horror and disgust I had just seen.

Sleep finally came, but it brought wild dreams of death and Elizabeth and my mother. When I suddenly awoke in a panic, my teeth were chattering, and my arms and legs were convulsing.

The dim light of the moon shone through the window into my bedroom. As my eyes flew open, the moonlight revealed the huge figure of the monster as he lifted up the curtains around my bed. He stared down at me with a horrible grin that forced wrinkles in his cheeks and stretched his ugly, black lips.

His jaws moved and he muttered some sounds that had no meaning. As he reached out to touch me, I jumped from my bed and rushed out the door of my apartment.

I fled down the stairs and into the courtyard. I hid there, weak, horrified, and bitterly disillusioned, for the rest of that dismal, rainy night.

Awaking in a Panic!

Wandering Aimlessly in Terror!

CHAPTER 6

Madness!

At six o'clock the next morning, I dragged my soaking wet body out of the courtyard. As I staggered through the streets of Ingolstadt, I had no idea where I was going or what I was doing.

I was terrified to return to my room and just as terrified to turn each corner, sick with fear that the monster might be there or anywhere, waiting for me.

After several hours of aimless wandering, I found myself in front of the inn that was the stopping-off place for coaches traveling in and out of the city. I don't know what made me stop at that very moment, but as I looked around, I saw the coach from Geneva approaching.

As the coach pulled to a stop, to my utter amazement, the passenger getting out was my dear friend, Henry Clerval.

"Victor!" he exclaimed. "What good luck to find you waiting here for me!"

I was delighted to see my closest friend. As we shook hands, I forgot for a moment the horror and misfortune I had lived though the previous night.

As we walked, arm in arm, towards my apartment, Henry explained why he was in Ingolstadt. "I finally persuaded my father that I needed to know more about the world than just how to be a bookkeeper in his business. So he agreed to let me attend the university."

"That's wonderful, Henry!" I told him. "I'm really happy to have you here with me. But do

A Surprise Visitor

you have news of my family?"

"They are all well and happy, but also worried at not having heard from you in a long time." He stopped walking then and stared hard at me. "I must confess, now that I see you, Victor, I'm worried too. You're so pale and thin. Are you ill?"

"Not ill," I explained, "just working very hard on a project which is now finished. At last, I can finally rest."

As we approached my apartment, my joy at seeing Henry was quickly replaced by fear. I began to tremble. What if the monster were still in my bedroom? I dreaded seeing him, but I dreaded even more the possibility that Henry might see him too!

I ran up the stairs ahead of Henry. A cold shiver came over me as I turned the doorknob and slowly opened the door. I breathed a great sigh of relief at finding my apartment empty, and I joyously led Henry inside.

My joy was so great that I began to laugh, a

Dreading What Might Be Upstairs

loud, wild laugh that stunned Henry. Then, when I began jumping over chairs and clapping my hands, he became truly frightened.

Taking me by the shoulders, he began to shake me. "For heaven's sake, Victor, you really *are* ill! What is it?"

My eyes began to roll wildly, and I pictured the monster walking in the door. "*He* is the cause!" I cried, pointing to nothing at the door. "Henry, please save me!"

As Henry shook me, I imagined it was the monster and I struggled furiously. I beat at him with my fists until I fell to the floor in a fit of convulsions.

How worried Henry must have been to see me this way! But I never knew it, for I was out of my mind for many months that followed. Henry never told my family of my illness but, instead, took care of me himself, day and night, with kindness and devotion.

The picture of the monster was before my eyes every minute of all those months. Henry

"*He* Is the Cause!"

paid no attention to these wild ravings, convinced it was my madness that caused them.

It was spring, more than five months later, before I began to recover. My gloom was disappearing, and I was becoming the same cheerful friend Henry had always known.

I knew how much I owed him, and I tried to express my gratitude. "Dear Henry, you spent this entire winter taking care of me when you could have been attending the university, which has been your dream for so many years. How can I ever repay you?"

"Just by taking care of yourself and getting completely well."

When that day arrived, I took Henry to the university and introduced him to my professors and to the other students.

Professor Waldman welcomed us warmly and told Henry, "Victor's astonishing progress has made us all very proud of him. Why, he's the top student at the university!"

Victor Takes Henry to the University.

While the professor's words were meant to praise me, they actually tortured me. For that "astonishing progress" was responsible for creating a terrible monster!

Henry had always been sensitive to my feelings, and he saw the agony in my eyes when Professor Waldman talked about me. Without questioning me about the cause of those feelings, Henry changed the subject, and the conversation was easier for me. Because I loved Henry as if he were my brother, I couldn't ever inflict on him the agony I was going through. And I'd be doing that by sharing my terrible secret with him.

When Henry visited my laboratory above my apartment, he saw how nervous I became when I spotted my instruments. He had no way of knowing the part they played in creating the monster. Again, without questioning me as to why I was so nervous, he quietly packed away the instruments and locked up the room.

By then, I had decided to give up my study

Packing Away Victor's Instruments

of science because of the horror it had brought into my life. But it wasn't my nature to remain idle, so I decided to remain at the university and join Henry studying Oriental languages.

We spent a relaxed, pleasant year together learning new languages, reading the beautiful, comforting books of Persian writers, and taking wonderful walking trips—often for weeks at a time—into the beautiful countryside around Ingolstadt.

I soon became the same happy person who had come to the university a few years before, with no sorrow and no care. The horror of the monster and my madness following his creation had been erased from my memory!

Wonderful Walking Trips

An Expected Letter Arrives.

CHAPTER 7

The First Murder!

One warm May morning, Henry and I had just returned from an invigorating, glorious walk in the countryside, when a letter from my father was delivered to me. I had been expecting it, for I was planning to visit my family in Geneva after my two years away.

I opened it eagerly and read:

Geneva, May 12

My dear son,

It is with sadness and tears that I call you back home. But first, I must prepare you for some terrible news before your arrival. Your darling little brother William is dead! That gentle, innocent child has been murdered!

I will not try to console you, but I will simply tell you what happened, as we know it.

Last Thursday evening, Elizabeth, your two brothers, and I went for a walk in the woods at Plainpalais, the park where you loved to run and play as a child. William and Ernest had been running ahead of us, playing hide and seek.

When it started getting dark, Elizabeth and I sat down on a bench to wait for the boys. In a while, Ernest returned, asking if we had seen William, who had gone to hide but had not returned.

We jumped up and immediately began to search. By nightfall, we hadn't found him, and Elizabeth returned home to alert our neighbors and get some torches to continue

Ernest Can't Find William.

our search for William.

At five o'clock in the morning, I made the gruesome discovery. I found William's cold, lifeless body in the grass, with the murderer's fingermarks still on his throat!

I tearfully carried him home and laid him on his bed. When Elizabeth bent over his lifeless body and saw his neck, she cried out, "Oh, God! I have murdered my darling child!" And she fainted in my arms.

When we revived her, she tearfully explained that earlier that day, William had begged to be allowed to wear her chain and locket, the one that belonged to your dear, dead mother and contained her picture. Elizabeth loved William so much, she couldn't refuse him anything.

When she discovered the locket missing from his neck, she assumed that robbery was the reason for his murder.

We have no trace of the murderer as yet. Elizabeth cannot stop crying and blames

Elizabeth Lets William Wear the Locket.

herself for William's death. We need you here, Victor, not to avenge the murder, but to help us heal our grieving hearts.

Your loving father,
Alphonse Frankenstein

I threw the letter on the table, covered my face with my hands, and began to cry uncontrollably.

Henry put his arm around my shoulders and asked, "My dear friend, what's wrong? What has happened to make you cry so bitterly?"

I couldn't speak and was barely able to catch my breath. In between sobs, I managed to point to the letter on the table.

Henry picked it up and began to read. He gasped, then tears gushed from his eyes as he, too, read the terrible news.

"My Dear Friend, What's Wrong?"

The City Gates Are Closed.

CHAPTER 8

Sighting the Monster

I hired a horse and carriage, and left immediately for Geneva. It was a sad journey, with my thoughts full of memories of my sweet, innocent brother and the horror my grieving family were all suffering.

As night came and I approached Geneva, gloom and fear replaced my sadness. It was after ten o'clock when I drove up to the gates of the city. In my grief, I had forgotten that the gates closed at ten. Since I couldn't enter the city until the next morning, I rented a room for the night at an inn in a nearby village on Lake Geneva.

I was too nervous to sleep, so I decided to rent a boat and sail across the lake. The woods of Plainpalais were on the other side, and I somehow needed to see the place where my brother was murdered.

A lightning storm was approaching over the mountains, and by the time I reached the shore, a heavy rain had begun to fall. Thunder burst with a deafening crash, and eerie flashes of lightning lit up the lake as if it were on fire.

No sooner had I pulled my boat up on shore than I caught sight of a figure on a gloomy mountainside. As the figure moved out from behind a thick clump of trees, I froze in my tracks and stared into the darkness.

The next flash of lightning lit up the figure. Its gigantic, hideous shape only confirmed my fears! It was the monster!

What was he doing here after all this time? Then I shuddered at another thought! I asked

A Gigantic, Hideous Shape Appears.

myself, "Could he have had anything to do with my brother's murder?"

No sooner did that question occur to me than I knew the answer. *Yes!* I knew for certain that only such a horrible monster could murder an innocent child!

My teeth began to chatter and my knees went weak. I leaned against a tree to keep from falling.

A moment later when I looked up, I saw the figure hurrying away. I started to follow him, but the next flash of lightning showed him climbing the steep rocks on the side of the mountain. Then he was gone, disappeared over the top.

I stood frozen against the tree, thinking back to the night two years ago when I had given life to this creature. I was filled with guilt as I now asked myself, "Did I turn a monster loose in the world so he could kill? And what other terrible crimes has he committed?"

Climbing the Steep Rocks and Disappearing

FRANKENSTEIN

I spent the night, cold and wet, on that hillside, agonizing on the horror I had created. When day dawned, I made my way to Geneva and to my father's house.

I considered alerting the police so that the monster could be tracked down. But what kind of story could I tell? Could I say that I, a university student, had created a monster and given life to it two years ago, then had seen that very monster on the side of the mountain just last night? Besides, who would believe such a strange tale from the lips of a man who had spent many months with a fever that was close to madness?

I knew that if someone came to *me* with such a story, I would say it was the ravings of a madman! Besides, what human could hope to stop or even catch a creature who was capable of climbing the sides of a mountain as the monster had done? . . . I had no answers, so I decided to remain silent.

Agonizing on His Horror!

Weeping Over a Sweet Brother's Picture

CHAPTER 9

A Sad Homecoming

It was five o'clock in the morning when I entered my father's house. I went straight to the library, telling the servants not to wake the family. I stood before the mantle-piece and gazed at the portrait of my dear mother, then below it, at one of William.

I clutched my sweet brother's picture to my heart and began to weep. At that moment, my brother Ernest entered the library and tearfully fell into my arms.

When we finally dried our eyes, I asked how my father and Elizabeth were bearing up.

"Father is managing fairly well, but Elizabeth has been inconsolable. She had been blaming herself for William's death until the real murderer was discovered—"

"The real murdered discovered!" I cried. "How can that be? I saw him just last night on the mountain, and he was still loose!"

"I don't know what you mean, Victor," replied my brother, looking puzzled. "The discovery of the murderer has just added to our misery, since it was our devoted servant girl, Justine Moritz."

"Justine?" I gasped. "That's impossible!"

"No one believed it at first. Elizabeth still doesn't. And actually, the evidence is very confusing. It seems one of the servants found our mother's locket in Justine's apron pocket—the locket that was stolen when William was murdered. Without coming to us with the locket first, the servant went to the police. They immediately came and arrested Justine. Her trial begins tomorrow."

The Police Arrest Justine Moritz.

"I'm certain she's innocent," I argued, "because I know who the real murderer is."

At that moment, my father and Elizabeth joined us, so there was no chance for Ernest to question me about what I had said.

After greeting me warmly but sadly, my father added to Ernest's explanation. "We all wanted very much to believe in Justine's innocence, not only because of all the years she has been with our family, but also because of her devotion to your late mother and to William. I hope and pray she will be acquitted. We must trust in the fairness of our judges and our court system."

Elizabeth waited until my father had finished speaking, then she tearfully pleaded with me, "Victor, you must find a way to help prove Justine's innocence. I love that girl and I know she couldn't kill anyone, certainly not the darling little boy she practically raised."

Elizabeth Pleads for Victor's Help.

Justine's Trial Begins.

CHAPTER 10

Justine Moritz—The Second Victim!

I went to the courthouse the next day with my father and Elizabeth. I wished more than anything that I could have confessed to the crime to avoid having Justine punished for it. But I had been in Germany at the time of the murder and anyone hearing my confession would probably think I was out of my mind.

The evidence against Justine was actually circumstantial—there was no real proof that she was guilty. She claimed that when she learned William was lost, she hurried to

Plainpalais to help in the search for him. After many hours when she tried to return home, it was after ten o'clock and the city's gates were already closed. So she waited in a barn in a nearby village until daylight. She thinks she fell asleep for a few minutes until some footsteps woke her.

Justine had no idea how the locket from William's neck had gotten into the pocket of her apron. She could only guess that someone had put it there.

"But who?" she begged the court. "I don't have an enemy in the world! And if someone killed William just to steal the locket, why did the murderer leave it in my pocket?"

Elizabeth came forward to testify to Justine's good character and to plead with the court. But I saw from the angry looks on the judges' faces that it was no use. They were already convinced that she was guilty.

I ran out of the courtroom, unable to face my own guilt. I was responsible for creating the

Justine Fell Asleep in a Barn.

monster who had committed this horrible crime!

A short while later, Elizabeth and my father staggered out, their faces white.

"Oh, Victor," sobbed Elizabeth, "it's even worse than we expected."

"Justine has confessed to the crime," my father explained sadly.

"No!" I cried. "I don't believe it!"

Just then, a court clerk came out and called to Elizabeth, "Oh, Miss Lavenza, the prisoner has asked to see you."

Elizabeth turned to me. "I must see Justine, even though she has confessed. But I can't go in alone. Please come with me."

I was tortured at the very thought of facing Justine, but I couldn't refuse.

We found the girl sitting on a pile of straw in her cell. Her hands were chained together and her head was resting on her knees. When she saw us, she threw herself at Elizabeth's feet and wept bitterly.

Learning of Justine's Confession

"Oh, Justine!" cried Elizabeth. "Why did you lie to us? I was so convinced of your innocence in spite of the evidence, but then I learned that you had confessed to the crime."

"I did confess," admitted Justine between sobs, "but the confession was a lie. I was forced to make the confession. They told me if I didn't confess, I could never enter heaven after my death. I was so frightened that I did what they said. But now I'm miserable. I could never die with you believing I had murdered our dear, sweet child! I've told you the truth and now I can go to my death peacefully. You know... and God knows... I'm innocent."

Seeing both women sobbing in each other's arms, I groaned in agony. I was helpless to comfort either one of these women who were my dear, lifelong friends.

Even though Elizabeth and I both tried desperately to change the judges' minds, it

Justine Swears She's Innocent.

did no good. At dawn of the following day, Justine Moritz was taken to the town square and hung as a murderess!

With horror and despair, I now counted two of my loved ones as the victims of my blind ambition and my terrible creation!

"What's the use of living?" I asked myself in desperation. "Suicide might be the answer for *me*, but how can I add more grief to the suffering Elizabeth and my father have been enduring?" Then, too, I didn't know what else the fiendish monster might be planning against my family. I had to protect them.

I decided then that I had to shake off my depression and take action myself. I swore, "One day, I shall track down this monster and come face to face with him. Then I shall make him pay for his terrible crimes!"

Preparing To Hang a Murderess!

The Alpine Air Lifts Victor's Spirits.

CHAPTER 11

Face to Face with the Monster

After Justine's death, I found it difficult to cope with my despair and depression at home in Geneva, so I went off by myself to the peaceful village of Chamounix.

After a month of calm, long walks along the glaciers in the beautiful Alpine valley and breathing in the fresh mountain air beneath Mont Blanc, I was able to relax during the day and sleep well at night.

One morning, though, I was awakened by a torrential rain that blocked out the beautiful view of the mountain I had from my room.

FRANKENSTEIN

Still, I refused to let the rain stop me from my daily climb to my favorite spot on the mountain. It was a place where I usually sat watching the glaciers as they slowly and silently traveled down the slopes.

As my mule carefully climbed the steep, winding path, the pouring rain continued pounding the valley below. I arrived at the top of the mountain at noon and decided to cross the glacier. Its three-mile width was covered with deep rifts, or cracks, in the ice, and it took me two hours to make my way across to the other side.

When the sun finally replaced the dismal rain, the icy mountain peaks began to glisten. The sparkling beauty around me changed my mood from gloom to joy.

Suddenly, from the other side of the glacier, I spotted the figure of a man—a huge figure of a man—approaching me at superhuman speed. Where I had trudged across the ice slowly and carefully, he ran and jumped over

Crossing the Three-Mile-Wide Glacier

the icy, dangerous surface.

I shivered as the shape came nearer, then trembled with rage and horror—it was the fiendish monster I had created two years earlier! I knew at that moment that I had to stay there and wait, to come face to face with him and tell him how much I despised him . . . and, if possible, to fight him to the death!

"Devil!" I shouted. "How dare you approach me! How I wish I could kill you with one blow and bring back to life the two people you have cruelly murdered!"

"I'm not surprised at your greeting. I expected it," he said calmly. "After all, everyone hates creatures as ugly as I am. But it's your fault that I'm this ugly. You created me this way."

I couldn't control my rage any longer, and I sprang at him, clawing at his hideous, yellow face.

But he was too quick and too strong for me. Grasping my arm in his powerful hold,

An Uncontrollable Rage!

he quietly replied, "Calm yourself, my creator. I beg you to hear my story before you try again to kill me. Remember, you made me larger and stronger than you."

"I don't want to hear anything you have to say, you vile creature!"

"How can I appeal to you, Victor Frankenstein? How can I convince you that I, too, have suffered? I have been miserable and alone, hated and scorned by all humans, adults and children, all because of you."

"And I hate and scorn myself for having created you!"

"Then you have a duty to hear what I have to say. Then if you still want to kill me, and if you *can*, then do it. Just remember it was you who created me."

"I curse the day I did it! I curse these hands that did it! Go! I can't bear to look at you a moment longer!"

The monster placed his hands over my eyes, saying, "Now you don't have to look at me."

"It Was You Who Created Me."

I flung his hands from my face and turned my back to him.

The monster reached out his hands as if to plead with me. "Then don't look at me. Just listen to my story and hear my request. If you grant it, I will leave you in peace. If you don't . . . well, we'll talk of that later."

I don't know if it was curiosity or fear or even pity that made me agree to listen to him. But whatever the reason, I decided I would. I turned to him and nodded my head.

He pointed across the glacier and said, "My story is too long for us to sit out here in the cold and talk. Please come with me. I know of a hut on that mountain."

He turned and started across the ice. I followed, trying hard to keep up with his speedy pace.

By the time I reached the hut, he was already inside lighting a fire. I seated myself close to it and listened as he began his tale.

Following the Monster Across the Glacier

"I Was a Helpless, Miserable Wretch."

CHAPTER 12

The Monster's Story Begins

When you first brought me to life, I was as helpless as a newborn baby, except that I could see, smell, hear, feel, and taste.

These sensations frightened me, so I came to your room, as a child would come to a father. But you ran away and left me, and I didn't know what to do.

I felt cold, so I covered myself with your cloak and went out into the night, a helpless, miserable wretch. I remember weeping as I walked through the streets, and by the time I reached a forest outside Ingolstadt, I was very tired and lay down on the damp ground near a brook.

I slept for several hours and awoke hungry and thirsty. I drank some water from the brook and ate a few berries I had found on the ground.

I spent a month in that forest and watched the sun and moon changing in the sky. I got to know the pleasant sounds that birds made as they flew over my head. I tried making those sounds myself, but I couldn't. I tried making other sounds with my mouth, but the harsh noises that came out frightened me.

As I began to explore outside the forest, I discovered a fire that some beggars must have left. I enjoyed the feelings of warmth and light it gave me, so I thrust my hand into the glowing coals. I quickly pulled it back with a cry of pain, puzzled why something that felt good could also give pain.

I examined the materials that made the fire burn and soon learned that branches did it,

A Painful Experience with Fire

with some help from the wind. I also discovered that nuts and roots tasted better if I cooked them in the fire before I ate them. But berries did not.

Soon, my supply of food was used up, and I had to leave the forest and my fire. I found myself in open country, where a great white blanket of something cold on the ground hurt and chilled my feet.

After three days of wandering without food or shelter, I came upon a small hut early one morning. I was hungry and tired when I dragged myself to the open door and went in. An old man was seated by a fire, cooking his breakfast. Seeing me in the room, he froze, then ran from the hut, screaming at the top of his lungs.

I ate the man's breakfast, then lay down on some straw and fell asleep.

I slept until noon, when the sun was high in the sky, then continued on my way, packing the leftover food from my breakfast in a pouch to

A Frightened Old Man

take with me.

After several hours of walking, I came to a village. I was awed by the many neat cottages and big houses, with vegetables in the gardens and milk and cheese on the window ledges. I entered one of these houses, only to horrify everyone there. Children ran from me screaming and women fainted.

The screams alerted everyone in the village, and people began coming at me from all sides, throwing rocks, swinging tools, and shouting horrible threats. I fled from the village and ran across the open fields until I had lost my pursuers.

Many hours later, I came upon a wooden shed that was attached to a neat cottage. I didn't dare enter the cottage after what had happened in the village, but I did crawl into the shed. It wasn't tall enough for me to stand up in, and I was barely able to sit inside. But I didn't mind. I was grateful to have a place to sleep, one which would also give me protection

Chased from a Village

from the snow and rain . . .and from attacks by people!

At daylight, I looked out to find myself surrounded by a pig sty and a pool of water. The side of the shed where I had crept in was the only open side. I covered this opening with wood and stones, which I could move aside to enter and leave. I also gathered some straw to make a bed.

Then I examined the planks of wood that formed the wall between the shed and the cottage. A large crack revealed an empty room on the cottage side.

I crept out of the shed and into the cottage, hoping to find something to eat. I found a loaf of bread and a cup with which I was able to drink the water from the pool.

I decided to make the shed my home until something or someone forced me to leave. It was a paradise compared to living out in open fields or in the forest.

As the days passed, I learned that three

Making an Entrance of Wood and Stones

people named De Lacey lived in the cottage: a young woman called Agatha, her brother Felix, and their old, blind father.

The family was very poor, and the two young people worked hard to feed and care for their beloved father, often going without food themselves so that the old man could eat. They had only a few vegetables from their garden and a little milk from their cow.

The kindness and love these people showed each other moved me deeply, and rather than steal any more food from them, I went out at night in search of berries and nuts in the forest. I also borrowed the young man's tools at night and cut wood for them. I left it at their door as a surprise and enjoyed their pleasure at their good fortune when they found it there each morning.

I was amazed to discover that they could bring fire into their cottage to cook their food and light up the room. At night, the young

A Pleasant Surprise for the De Laceys

man and woman used this fire on a candle to read to the old man. The words they read were like those they spoke, and they read them from things called books.

As the days, weeks, and months went by, I taught myself to speak those words. I hoped that one day I would be able to introduce myself to them, and I wanted more than anything to be able to speak to them in their words. Perhaps that way they would overlook my ugliness. . . . Oh, yes, I had learned just how ugly I was when I saw my reflection in the water in the pond.

One morning, a beautiful lady arrived at the cottage on horseback. Felix greeted her warmly and called her Safie. Safie was his fiancee, and was here to marry him. She had come from a faraway country called Turkey and didn't speak the same language as the family.

Felix and Agatha spent the weeks following Safie's arrival teaching her to speak and read

Safie Arrives To Marry Felix.

their language. Through the cracks in the wood, I listened to them and learned to speak many of their words too.

On one of my trips into the forest, I had found a suitcase containing some clothing and several books. I used those books to teach myself to read, along with Safie.

I spent the winter and spring enjoying my simple life and taking pleasure in the happy family I felt so close to. I was proud of the progress I was making in speaking all the words the family spoke and in reading them as well.

But what good were words when I had no one to speak them to? Would I ever be able to face people and not have them run from my ugliness? Would I ever have someone look at me with expressions of love, as I saw with Felix and Safie? Would I ever have friends or a family? Even the man I considered my father, you—Victor Frankenstein, ran from my wretchedness!

Learning To Read

Another event strengthened my bitter feelings against you. When I first came to my shed, I found your notebook in the pocket of the cloak I had taken from your bedroom when I ran from there years ago. At first, it had no meaning for me, but once I could read, I learned of your work and your thoughts before you began creating me and while you were doing it. Yes, I learned of your horror at seeing my hideous body when you were finished.

Why did you make me so hideous that you turned away in disgust? How I curse the day you gave me life! How I curse you!

But my bitterness was softened when I thought of the kindly De Laceys, who, I was certain, would befriend me and overlook my ugliness when I told them my story and when they came to know me as a good person.

Still, even though I longed for kindness and sympathy from them, I put off introducing myself to them, for fear that they, too, would turn away from me in horror.

Bitter at Learning Victor's Thoughts

FRANKENSTEIN

By the time I had been in my shed for a year, I started planning how to introduce myself to the family. I decided to enter the cottage when the old man was alone, since his blindness would prevent him from seeing my ugliness. Then, I reasoned, when his children met me, they would see that their father liked me and they would too.

One morning, after the young people had gone to a fair in the village, I saw my chance. I left my shed, and with my knees shaking and my hands trembling, I went to the front door and knocked.

When De Lacey called, "Come in," I took a deep breath and opened the door. I introduced myself as a traveler in need of some rest, and the old man welcomed me. He even offered to share his bits of food with me.

We spent several hours talking about many things and agreed how important it is for a man to have friends. I truly believed that the old man had become my friend, and I was on

A Friend at Last?

my knees, grasping his hand in gratitude when the cottage door opened.

I can't begin to describe the horror of the young people at seeing me. Safie ran out the door and Agatha fainted. Felix lunged at me and, with superhuman strength, pulled me away from his father as I clung to the old man's knees.

I fell to the floor, and Felix began beating me with a stick. I could have torn him apart with my bare hands, but I didn't. I just ran from the cottage in despair and didn't stop until nightfall, when I reached a thick forest.

I was alone in the world again, with no friends, no human beings to talk to. My rage knew no limits! My brain wanted only revenge . . . revenge against the world . . . and revenge against you, my creator!

Felix Protects His Father.

Traveling Only At Night

CHAPTER 13

A Confession of Murder

I set out to find you, remembering from your notebook that a place called Geneva was your home. Since geography had been part of the lessons Felix had taught Safie, which I learned as well, I knew I had to head in a southwest direction.

My heart was filled with hate. You gave me a body, a mind, and feelings, then cast me out to be scorned by the world. I swore I'd repay the world and you too!

I traveled only at night, with winter fast approaching. Snow fell all around, and the ground was icy under my feet. But I continued on all winter, in spite of the weather. With each step, my rage against you grew!

I traveled that way, avoiding villages and sleeping in open fields, until spring. When I reached the Swiss border, I decided to enjoy the warm days and travel in daylight, but keeping hidden by following a path through the forest.

One day, the path crossed a river. As I neared it, I heard voices. I hid behind a tree as a young girl came running by. She was laughing as if playfully hiding from someone behind her. Suddenly, her foot slipped and she fell into the river.

The force of the current quickly pulled her out to the rapids. I jumped in and, with great exertion, saved her. I dragged the unconscious child to shore and had just revived her when a man—her father, I imagined—tore her from my arms and rushed back towards the forest with her.

Rescuing a Drowning Child

FRANKENSTEIN

As I started to follow them, he placed her on the ground, then turned to me, a gun in his hand. He took aim, then fired several shots. I sank to the ground, writhing in pain from the bleeding flesh and bone in my shoulder.... This, then, was my reward for saving the child's life!

I spent the next few weeks in the forest, healing my wounds and eager for revenge. Finally, I was well enough to continue on.

It was early evening two months later when I reached the woods outside Geneva. I was tired and hungry as I sat down under a tree, trying to decide just how I would find you and confront you.

I had just begun to doze when a beautiful young child came running towards me. A glimmer of hope flickered in my heart. Here was an innocent boy who probably hadn't learned to be horrified at ugliness like grown-ups were. Perhaps he could become my friend.

I reached out and grabbed the boy as he

A Reward for Saving a Child's Life

ran by. As soon as he saw me, he covered his eyes and began to scream. I pulled his hands away from his face and said gently, "I'm not going to hurt you."

"Let me go, you ugly monster!" he cried. "Let me go or I'll call my father. He's an important man and he'll punish you. His name is Alphonse Frankenstein."

"Frankenstein!" I shrieked. "You belong to my enemy. Now I'll have my revenge. You will be my first victim!"

The child continued to struggle and scream terrible words at me. I grabbed his throat to quiet him, but the next moment he lay dead at my feet. I realized then that this would bring misery to you, and I was glad!

As I gazed down at the boy, I spotted a locket around his neck. I picked it up and stared at a picture of a beautiful woman. I knew that a woman of such beauty would never look at me...and my rage at you returned once more.

"My Rage at You Returned Once More."

I left the murder spot then, still holding the locket, and went on towards Geneva. I soon came to a barn, where I found a young woman asleep on some straw. For a moment, I was terrified that she would waken and see me, and surely be horrified at my ugliness too. And later, she could probably identify me as the boy's murderer.

Even though I had no way of knowing for certain she would do that, I decided to make her suffer anyway. So, I put the locket in the pocket of her apron, knowing that when it was found, it would point to her as the murderer.

Once that was done, I hid and waited until the boy's body was discovered and followed everyone into the city. Later, I learned the girl had been arrested for the murder.

Then I began wandering through Geneva and through these mountains, waiting for the moment when I would come face to face with you. And now, at last, that moment is here!

Blaming the Murder on a Young Woman

"What Do You Want of Me?"

CHAPTER 14

A Terrible Promise

The creature finished his story, then stared at me, waiting for my reaction.

I was bewildered. One part of me was enraged by his crimes, while another part of me pitied him for the cruel way he had been treated by everyone, including me.

I looked straight into those hideous yellow eyes and demanded, "So now that we're face to face, what do you want of me?"

"I want a friend ... someone who won't be revolted by my ugliness, but who will be as ugly as I am ... someone who will understand me and have sympathy for me. I want you to create that friend . . . create a wife for me, just as you created me."

My rage exploded. "Never!" I cried. "I will never create another evil creature to commit the same terrible crimes you have committed. You may torture me or threaten me, but I will never do it."

"I wasn't threatening you," he said in a calm voice. "I was trying to reason with you. Please understand that I tried to love my fellow beings, but all they did was hate me, just as you have done."

"I still can't do it . . . I won't do it!"

The monster then began to rage, twisting his face into forms too horrible for human eyes to look at. "I swear I'll destroy you just as you have destroyed me . . . unless you agree to my demands!" he warned.

I turned away, but the monster pleaded again. "If only I could be treated with a little kindness from just one person, I would repay

"I Swear I'll Destroy You!"

that kindness to all mankind."

I was moved by his argument. He was a creature who had feelings...deep feelings. And didn't I owe him something since I had created him?

Sensing my anger soften, he continued. "If you agree to make this woman for me, no one will ever see either of us again. We will go away, far across the ocean, to an uninhabited part of South America and live out our lives without doing any harm to man or beast anywhere."

I felt compassion and sympathy for him and for the life I had forced on him. But then, when I turned back to look at him, I felt my horror and hatred return. Then reason took over and I figured that by doing what he asked, I would be protecting all mankind from the evil he was capable of inflicting.

Finally, after a long silence, I said, "I will do as you ask, but only if you swear that as soon as I have created this woman, you both will

Pleading for Compassion

leave Europe forever."

"I swear that you will never see us again!" he cried. "Now go to your laboratory immediately and begin your work. I shall be watching you all the time, even though you won't see me. You can be sure that I will reappear when the woman is finished."

Then he turned and left, perhaps afraid that I would change my mind. I watched him descend the mountain faster than any eagle could fly over it. Soon, he had disappeared in the snow and ice.

It was dusk when I started down the mountain, weeping bitterly and raging at myself. We had been talking the entire day, and it took me the entire night to make my way down into the valley.

I reached Chamounix at dawn and left immediately for Geneva. I knew I had to begin my dreaded work as soon as possible.

Weeping Bitterly Over Dreaded Work

Trying To Get Up Courage To Begin

CHAPTER 15

Beginning a Second Creature

My wild appearance frightened my family, and they became even more alarmed when I refused to answer any of their questions about what had happened to me. I couldn't tell them. I knew only that because I loved them, I had to save them from the monster.

Days and weeks went by, and I couldn't seem to get up enough courage to begin my work. The very thought of it filled me with horror, even though I feared the fiend's revenge if he were disappointed. But I also knew this new work would require many months of study before I could even begin.

During these weeks, my health began to improve, and my father was delighted. He came to me one day and said, "It is time to end our mourning and go on with our lives, my son. You know it was your mother's fondest wish, and mine as well, that you and Elizabeth would marry one day. I hope this can happen soon, as I'm growing older and I'm not in the best of health."

"Father, I love Elizabeth and want to marry her," I assured him. But my mind was racing with thoughts of the promise I had made, a promise that had to be kept first. I had to create a wife for the creature before I could be assured of happiness with my own wife. If I didn't, I might be bringing untold misery on my family and on myself.

During my weeks at home, I had read about some new studies on the human body being done in England. It seemed a good idea to do my work there rather than in my father's

Reminding Victor of His Mother's Wish

house, where I would fear a thousand horrible accidents . . . or my reactions . . . or even my loss of sanity during my loathsome task. No, I had to do this work far away from the people I loved.

So, I told my father, "I still have some scientific studies I need to complete in England, and after that, I would like to spend some time traveling in order to regain my health completely. Then I will certainly look forward to marrying Elizabeth."

My father and Elizabeth were delighted to see my new attitude and encouraged my trip. But because they still had some concerns about my health, they quietly arranged for my dear friend, Henry Clerval, to travel to England with me.

Henry and I left Geneva at the end of September and traveled through France, Germany, and Holland before crossing the Channel into England.

A stay of four months in London was enough

Victor and Henry Leave for England.

time for me to learn about the new studies on the human body and enough time as well for me to buy all the materials and medical instruments I would need.

After that, we spent the next two months traveling through the English lake country and visiting friends in Scotland. By then, I realized that I had already been putting off starting my work for too many months. I began to fear what would happen if the monster learned of my delay. Was he planning some revenge on my family? Or was he following Henry and me? I began to panic.

I became so possessed that I feared days when no letter came from my father or Elizabeth. I became so possessed that I often refused to leave Henry's side for a moment and followed him everywhere.

Finally, I made my decision how and where to start. First, I told Henry, "We've been enjoying our friends here in Scotland for a while now, and I want you to spend more time here.

Buying Medical Instruments

I, however, need some time by myself, perhaps a month or two. Then, when I return, I'll be the old Victor you've always known. I'll be much better company, I promise you."

"Really, Victor," he protested, "you know I'd much rather be with you, no matter where you're going. But if you need to be alone, I'll respect your wishes. Just hurry back."

I left Henry then and headed for the Orkney Islands, a barren island group off the coast of Scotland. I chose an island that was little more than a rock, with only five people living on it.

I rented a small, miserable hut. It had two squalid rooms, a thatched roof that had fallen in on the house, plaster that was hanging away from the walls, a door that was off its hinges, and a few pieces of broken furniture.

I had the necessary repairs made and set up one room as a laboratory. Then I finally settled down to begin my work.

A Place to Begin Work

As the woman's body took shape, however, I began to hate my work more and more each day. Sometimes, I couldn't force myself to go into my laboratory for days at a time. Other times, I worked day and night to finish a particular part of the body.

I thought back to the first creature I had made and recalled how enthusiastic I was, an enthusiasm that blinded me to the horror of what I was doing. But now, I was doing it in cold blood, and I could barely look at my hands as they worked.

I became restless. I grew nervous. I raised my eyes constantly, fearing to see the monster appear in front of me.

Still, my work was proceeding well. I was close to completing it. Why, then, did such a sickening sense of foreboding fill my heart? ... This foreboding, this feeling that something evil was about to happen, began to haunt me day and night.

The Woman's Body Is Close to Completion.

Another Evil Creature?

CHAPTER 16

The Monster's Threat

One evening as I sat in my laboratory, I thought again, as I often did, of the time when I was forming my first creature three years ago. I remembered that I had no idea at that time just what kind of evil fiend he would turn out to be.

Then, suddenly, a frightening thought occurred to me! "I have no way of knowing what this new creature will be like! What if she turns out to be ten thousand times more terrible than her husband? What if she delights in evil or even murder as he has done? What if she refuses to go away to South America with him as he promised? What if they hate each other, he because she is so ugly, and she because of his ugliness as well?"

But then an even more horrifying thought came to me. "Suppose they *do* get along together and go off to South America, what will happen if they have children? And what if these children are evil like their father and terrorize mankind"?

Suddenly, for the first time, the terrible consequences of my promise struck me with horror. And it was at that very moment that I looked up to discover the fiend's face at the window. An evil, ghastly smile spread across his lips as he gazed from me to his partly finished bride.

That ghastly smile and the maddening gaze made me realize that he was planning some new evil. How could I ever have been insane enough to promise to create this being!

My rage intensified until I was nearly out

A Ghastly Smile That Promises Evil!

of control and out of my mind. I took hold of the partly finished creature and began tearing it to pieces! Arms, legs, body parts flew everywhere, scattering all over the floor of the laboratory.

I took one last look at the monster at the window, then rushed out the door, leaving the hated laboratory behind me.

The monster howled in despair and shook his fists at my fleeing back. Then he turned and disappeared into the night.

Once my rage subsided, I spent the next several hours sitting at my bedroom window, staring at the calm sea. A few fishing boats were gently rocking in the water, and the friendly voices of the fishermen reached my ears.

Suddenly, I spotted a boat paddling furiously towards the shore. The bright moon lit up a figure as it beached the boat close to my house and jumped out.

I began to tremble again, knowing without

Tearing the Creature to Pieces!

a doubt who it was. I wanted to flee, but I was frozen to my chair.

Moments later, my door was flung open and the monster stumbled in. "Why did you break your promise?" he demanded. "Why did you destroy your work and destroy my hopes for a wife after all this time?"

"Leave me!" I cried. "I broke my promise because I can never again create a being as ugly or as evil as you, one who delights in murdering innocent people!"

"Ugly, yes! Evil, yes . . . now!" he exploded. "But also powerful . . . more powerful than you, my creator."

"Yes, you are more powerful than I am, but your threats don't frighten me."

Gnashing his teeth in anger, he warned, "I'll never let you be happy while I'm alone and miserable. I'll have my revenge on you. From this day on, revenge against you will be my only reason for living!"

"Get out, you devil!" I screamed.

"Why Did You Break Your Promise?"

"I'll go," he said quietly, with evil in his voice. "But remember, I'll be with you always, ready for my revenge. And...I will be with you on your wedding night."

I lunged at him furiously, but he was too fast for me as he ran from the house and jumped into his boat. Moments later, I saw him shooting across the water with the speed of an arrow.

I stood on the shore, burning with rage as his words rang in my ears. *"I will be with you on your wedding night."*

So that was when he planned to kill me. I wasn't afraid for myself, but I couldn't bring such pain and sorrow to my dear Elizabeth. Tears filled my eyes. They were the first tears I had shed in many months.

At that moment, I made up my mind that I wouldn't let my enemy kill me...not without a bitter struggle.

Burning with Rage!

A Hateful Room!

CHAPTER 17

The Murderer Strikes Again!

The following morning, I decided to leave the island and rejoin Henry. I knew from his letters that he was anxious to see me and continue our travels together.

But before I left, there was one disagreeable task I had to perform. I had to pack up my medical instruments and clean up the laboratory.

When I opened the door, the scene in that hateful room filled me with disgust. The remains of the partly finished creature lay scattered on the floor. I couldn't leave them there to be found by any island people who might come by. They would surely be horrified, and then suspicious of what I had been doing there.

So, after washing and packing away all my instruments, I gathered the body parts and tossed them into a large suitcase. I then took the suitcase down to the beach and added some heavy stones to weigh the whole thing down. I fastened the lid, then hid the suitcase in a thick clump of bushes.

I stayed in my hut until night fell, then I returned to the beach and loaded the suitcase into my little skiff. As I sailed out a few miles from shore, I saw several fishing boats heading in towards the island. The men recognized me and waved, but I steered away from them and from the island.

I waited until the bright moon was hidden by a thick cloud, and under the cover of a moment of darkness, I tossed the suitcase into the sea.

Weighing Down the Suitcase

FRANKENSTEIN

As the suitcase gurgled and sank, I felt a new calm come over me. This calm, combined with the gentle rocking of the sea, made me so relaxed that I fell asleep.

I slept soundly all night. It wasn't until the following morning, when the sun was high in the sky, that I finally awakened.

A strong wind was blowing, and the waves were pounding hard against my little skiff. I realized that while I had been asleep, the wind had blown my boat far from the island where I lived. I was nowhere near any land and, I feared, probably somewhere out in the Atlantic Ocean.

The hours passed and by late afternoon, the sea became very rough. I was beginning to suffer from thirst and from the heat, and from the fear that I would die here in the middle of the ocean, either by drowning or from starvation.

Just when daylight was beginning to fade, I spied some land to the south. My one sail

Lost at Sea!

wasn't strong enough for me to maneuver the boat. So I made a second sail from my shirt and eagerly steered toward the small town that appeared to have a good harbor.

I was busy tying up the boat when several townspeople came up to me and crowded around me. I was surprised that no one offered to help me, since I was exhausted, ragged, and dried out from the sun. Instead, they began whispering to each other.

Puzzled at their behavior, I called out, "Good people, would you be so kind as to tell me where I am?"

A fisherman stepped forward. "You'll know soon enough," he said harshly. "You may not like this place, but no one here will really care if you do or not."

I was surprised at such rudeness from strangers, but I became more concerned when I saw angry frowns on every face in the crowd. "I hardly expected Englishmen to greet strangers in such an unfriendly way," I told

Puzzled at the Townspeople's Behavior

them indignantly.

"I don't know much about the way the English greet strangers," said the man. "But you're in Ireland now, and we Irish hate villains."

"Villains?" I gasped. "What do you mean? I haven't done anything villainous."

"That's not for us to decide. You'd better come with us to Mr. Kirwin, our town magistrate. He'll want to question you about the murder of a gentleman here last night."

I was puzzled, but very certain that I could explain how I wasn't involved in any murder that took place here. So, although I was exhausted and hungry, I put my shirt back on and followed the crowd to Mr. Kirwin's house. Little did I know the horror that was about to overwhelm me!

The magistrate was a kindly old man who seemed fair as he questioned the crowd that led me to his house.

The fisherman spoke first. "I was out in my

Following the Crowd to the Town Magistrate

boat last night, sir, with my son. When the wind began to blow too strong, we pulled into shore. As we were beaching our boat, I struck my foot against something hard.

"By the light of my lantern I saw that it was a body, a handsome young man, I'd say about twenty-five years old. His body was still warm, so we weren't sure if he was dead or just unconscious. We carried him to a nearby house and tried to revive him, but it was no use. He was dead.

"At first, I figured he had drowned and that his body had been washed up on shore. But then we realized that his clothes were dry. So he hadn't been in the water.

"Then when we saw black fingermarks on his neck, we knew he'd been strangled!"

I hadn't paid much attention to the man's story at first, but when he told of the fingermarks on the man's neck, I felt my blood run cold. My hands began to tremble and my legs collapsed under me. I had to clutch at a chair

Finding a Body on the Beach

to keep from falling.

The magistrate looked at me strangely, but then turned his attention to a woman in the crowd and asked what she knew.

The woman explained, "You know, sir, I live near the beach. A while before I heard about the murder, I saw a man in a boat push off from that part of the shore where the body was found, but I didn't recognize him."

Turning to me, Mr. Kirwin said, "Since you were found on the shore with a boat, it will be necessary for you to come with me to see the body."

I figured he wanted to see how I would react to the body, since I had become so upset when the fisherman described the finger-marks on the man's throat. So, I followed the magistrate and a few of the men to the village inn. We made our way to a bare back room that was empty except for a plain wooden coffin in the center.

Then came the terrible moment...a

"Come with Me To See the Body."

moment almost too terrible to talk about even now without shuddering in agony. For as I was led up to the coffin to see the lifeless body inside, I cried out in horror!

That lifeless body stretched out before me was Henry Clerval!

I gasped for breath and threw myself on his cold body. Sobs tore from my chest as I cried, "Have my evil schemes killed you too, my dear friend? I have already been responsible for the deaths of two others. How many more victims will that demon claim as he claimed you, Henry, my lifelong friend—"

I couldn't continue. My body began to convulse in agony, and I slumped to the floor, unconscious.

Henry Clerval—the Second Victim!

Delerious with Fever in Prison

CHAPTER 18

Imprisoned for Murder!

I spent the next two months in prison, delirious with fever and very near death. Mr. Kirwin later told me that my ranting and raving made no sense to the jailers who heard me and were convinced I was insane. I continually accused myself of murdering my brother, my friend Justine, and now Henry.

I kept begging everyone around me to help me destroy someone I called "the fiend." I often had nightmares, during which I would scream in terror that the fiend's fingers were on my neck, strangling me!

FRANKENSTEIN

When the fever left me and I regained my sanity, I found myself in a wretched cell with barred windows. An old woman was asleep in a chair beside my bed.

"Who are you?" I asked, waking her.

"I was hired to help you get well," she snapped, "although I don't know why you'd want to get well, not when they get done punishing you for the man they say you murdered."

I turned away from this unfeeling woman, but then realized that no one would care much about a murderer, except perhaps the hangman who would get paid for hanging me.

I soon learned, however, that Mr. Kirwin had been very kind to me during my illness. He had sent a doctor to treat me and the nurse to care for me. He came to see me often, although it was difficult for him to listen to the ravings of someone he considered a murderer.

One day, when I was strong enough to sit up

"Who Are You?"

in a chair, Mr. Kirwin entered my cell. Pulling up a chair next to mine, he asked, "Is there anything you need to make you more comfortable?"

I looked into his kind, sympathetic eyes and replied, "I thank you, sir, but only death can make me comfortable. Only death can free me from my misery."

"Don't lose hope, my boy. From papers I found in your pocket, I learned who you are and who your family is in Geneva."

I began to tremble at the mention of my family. "Good God!" I gasped. "Has anything happened to them? Has there been another murder?"

"Your family is well," Mr. Kirwin assured me, then added with a smile, "and you have a visitor here to see you."

I feared the worst—the fiend was here to torture me with the story of Henry's murder! I covered my eyes and cried out, "No! Take him away! Don't let him come in!"

"Don't Let Him Come In!"

Mr. Kirwin stood up and stared down at me in shock. "Perhaps you *are* guilty, after all, Victor. I should think that seeing your father would please you."

"My father!" I cried.

Mr. Kirwin then went to the door and led my father into my cell.

My joy at seeing him was surpassed only by his reassurances that Elizabeth and Ernest were also well. Because I was still so weak, he didn't stay too long during that first visit.

During the next month, Mr. Kirwin and my father gathered evidence from the peasants at Orkney Island proving that I was there, not in Ireland, the night that Henry was murdered. As a result, the charges against me were dismissed, and I was released from prison.

I knew I had to return to Geneva immediately to protect the people I loved and to destroy the monster I had created! My father

Overjoyed at Seeing His Father

was concerned about my making such a long trip so soon after my illness. I was still a shattered wreck. My strength was gone, my body was nothing more than a skeleton, and I still suffered from fits of fever. But I was so insistent on leaving Ireland and returning to Geneva that my father finally agreed.

He had heard my strange-sounding ravings many times during his month with me in Ireland. And even though he attributed them to my fever, he was puzzled why I continually accused myself of the murders of William, Justine, and Henry.

"My dear son," he told me, "I beg you not to ever make such accusations again. You are not responsible for these terrible deaths."

I remained silent, not wishing to burden my father with my tale of horror, although I wished more than anything in the world to be able to confide my secret to another human being.

"My Dear Son, You Are Not Responsible . . ."

A Letter Reminds Victor of a Threat.

CHAPTER 19

A Joyous Wedding

On the day of our departure from Ireland, I received a letter from Elizabeth. She reassured me of her love, but offered to release me from my promise to marry her if I no longer wanted to after so many years.

This certainly wasn't true. I loved her as much as ever and wanted nothing more in life than to marry her. But her letter reminded me of the threat I had put out of my mind . . . the monster's threat—*"I will be with you on your wedding night."*

I put the letter down and thought, "If that

is the night the monster has chosen for my death, so be it. There will be a deadly struggle between us. If the fiend wins, I'll be dead, and so at peace. If I win, the fiend will be dead and I'll be a free man."

I also decided that on the day after our wedding, I would confess my terrible secret to Elizabeth, for I didn't want to have any secrets from her, no matter how terrible they were.

As soon as my father and I arrived back in Geneva, we began making plans for the wedding. At first, Elizabeth was overjoyed at the news, but she soon began to worry about my continuing fits of depression and grief.

I tried to explain to her that something *was* troubling me deeply, and I hoped she would be comforted when I added, "I don't want to burden you with those troubles now when we're so busy with our wedding plans. But I promise to tell you everything the day after you become my wife."

Worried Over Victor's Depression

During the week preceding our wedding, I began making plans to defend myself against the fiend. I carried a dagger and pistols with me at all times, and was always on my guard against any trickery.

As the wedding day neared, I became calmer and began to treat the threat as a delusion, not important enough for me to worry about.

The ceremony was performed at our family home, with a large party following it. Every moment of the wedding brought great happiness to Elizabeth and me, and to my father as well.

We planned to spend our honeymoon at a villa that Elizabeth had inherited from her family. It sat on the shores of beautiful Lake Como in northern Italy. We would be crossing Lake Geneva first and spending our wedding night at an inn in the town of Evian before starting our land journey down into Italy.

The beauty of that ride across the lake on a

Defenses Against the Fiend

glorious summer day, with snowy Mont Blanc in the background, filled us both with joy. But then I noticed that joy was replaced by a look of fear in Elizabeth's eyes.

I took her hand in mine and smiled down at her, trying hard to reassure her that everything was fine, that I was happy and proud to have her as my wife. But in my heart, I wondered if she was dreading the confession of my terrible secret . . . the secret I had promised to reveal the following day.

That following day was actually only a few hours away, for the sun was setting as we landed on the shores of Evian. That sunset seemed to bring my own fears back to me, and I heard that horrible voice again. *I shall be with you on your wedding night.*

Starting on a Honeymoon

Victor is Filled with a Thousand Fears.

CHAPTER 20

A Wedding Night Victim!

As night fell, a heavy rain began to beat down on the little inn. From the window of our sitting room, we watched the wind and rain kick up the waves in the lake. The eerie gusts and the pounding storm filled me with a thousand fears once again. My only comfort was the pistol hidden inside my shirt.

Elizabeth silently watched the terror build up on my face until she finally asked, "What are you so terribly frightened of, my dear Victor?"

"It's only this dreadful night, my love," I tried to reassure her. "Once it passes, everything will be fine."

Then I realized that if the fiend and I were to confront each other that night, I couldn't let Elizabeth witness it. So I begged her, "Please, my dear, go into our bedroom and lie down to rest. You've had a tiring day. I'll join you shortly."

Once Elizabeth had left the sitting room, I walked through every inch of every hallway of the inn, inspecting every corner where the fiend might hide. But there was no trace of him.

I was beginning to believe that some real stroke of luck had prevented his carrying out his threat . . . when I suddenly heard a dreadful scream coming from our bedroom!

In that instant, I realized the true meaning of the monster's threat! I rushed into the bedroom, only to be frozen at the doorway by the horrifying sight before me!

Inspecting Every Corner of the Inn

There, thrown across the bed, was my dear, sweet Elizabeth, unmoving and lifeless. Her head was hanging down over the side of the bed, with her hair partly hiding a pale face now frozen into a twisted mask of terror.

I felt the blood leave my body, and I collapsed to the floor, unconscious!

When I came to, I was on a sofa in our sitting room, surrounded by the horror-stricken people from the inn. I jumped up and ran back to our bedroom, where Elizabeth's body had been placed in a more peaceful position on the bed. Her face and neck had been covered over with a cloth.

I tore the cloth away and took her in my arms. While she appeared to only be asleep, her cold, stiff body confirmed that she was dead ... that and the murderous black fingermarks on her neck!

As I lifted my eyes in agony to appeal to the heavens, I discovered a hideous, grinning face at the open window. That evil grin seemed to

The Monster's Threat is Carried Out!

be mocking me as a fiendish finger pointed at my dear Elizabeth's body.

"I have had my revenge, oh master," he cackled hoarsely. "I am here, as I swore I would be . . . on your wedding night. I have taken away from you all your hopes for happiness, just as you took away mine!"

I rushed toward the window, pulling the pistol from my shirt as I ran. I fired off several shots, but he was much too quick.

Leaping from window, he ran towards the lake and dove into the water.

The shots from my pistol had brought a crowd into the room. We rushed to the lake, and while some spread out in boats and with nets, others searched the woods nearby. Many hours later, we were forced to give up the search. The murderer had escaped!

Utterly exhausted, I returned to the inn. There was nothing more I could do for Elizabeth, but if the fiend were planning to harm my family, I had to return home immediately!

"I Have Had My Revenge, Oh Master."

Dying in Victor's Arms

A Worldwide Search Begins

I returned to Geneva to find my father and brother alive and safe. But the sad news I brought proved to be the final blow to my father's poor health. He simply couldn't go on living with the grief of the horrible deaths of his loved ones. Only a few days after my return, he took his last breath and died in my arms.

This was the final blow for me as well. The deaths of William, Justine, Henry, Elizabeth, and now my father were too much for my weakened mind to cope with. I went completely mad and had to be locked up in a hospital for the insane for many months.

When I finally awoke in my right mind, I was filled with an even greater desire for revenge than ever before. And this time, I was determined to do something about it.

I tried asking for help from the police in Geneva. I told my whole story to a judge, not leaving out any detail. Although he seemed to believe me, he decided that the superhuman powers of the monster, plus the time that had passed since the murders, made it impossible for anyone to catch him.

That left me with only one choice—to go after the fiend myself, even if it meant spending the rest of my life doing it!

Gathering together all the money I had, I made plans to leave Geneva. But I asked myself, "Where should I go? The monster could be anywhere on the face of the earth."

I began wandering through the city, and as night fell, I found myself at the cemetery

Telling His Story to a Judge

where William, Elizabeth, and my father were buried. I knelt at their graves and called out my vow to the heavens. "I swear I will pursue the fiend who took the lives of these loving, innocent people and make him pay for his crimes!"

The stillness of the night was broken by a loud, fiendish laugh that deafened me as it echoed from mountain to mountain. When the laughter died away, a hated, familiar voice whispered, "I have had my revenge on you, just as I said I would. I have made your life miserable, just as you did mine. And you will live to be even more miserable!"

I darted to the spot where the voice had come from, but the fiend had fled with a speed that no human could hope to match.

From that moment on, the pursuit had begun. With only a few clues to go on, I spent many months following the fiend throughout every country in Europe and Africa, and finally up into Russia.

A Vow To Make the Fiend Pay for His Crimes!

FRANKENSTEIN

Sometimes, frightened peasants who had sighted him pointed out his route. Other times, he, himself, left clues to guide me. He seemed to want me to suffer the agony of getting close and not capturing him.

I found messages from him cut into the bark of trees or scratched into rocks. The more he taunted me, the more determined I was to continue on and have my revenge.

Heading north in Russia, I found his last message: "Wrap yourself in furs and prepare to suffer on a long journey. Your suffering will satisfy my eternal hatred of you."

I bought a sledge and dog team, and crossed the snows of Russia with amazing speed. I was only a day behind him when I reached a tiny village and learned that the night before, a huge monster had attacked the villagers. Threatening them with guns and pistols, he had stolen their entire supply of food for the winter, plus a sledge and dog team for crossing the ice.

The Monster's Last Message

FRANKENSTEIN

The villagers warned me, "Don't follow him! He headed out across the frozen sea. There's no land at all in that direction. You'll both be destroyed, if not by the ice breaking under you and drowning you, then by the cold freezing you to death!"

But I wouldn't take their warning. I had to have my revenge at any cost!

I don't know how many weeks or months I spent on the ice, suffering unbelievable cold, thirst, hunger, and exhaustion. Then one morning, I reached the top of an ice mountain and discovered a dark spot moving on the frozen sea below.

I lifted my telescope to my eye and cried out in triumph when I saw that the spot was a sledge. Seated on it was a hideous shape I knew so well. Tears filled my eyes and I wept for joy.

I followed the fiend for two days, but I wasn't able to get any closer than the mile that separated us.

The Villagers Warn Victor.

FRANKENSTEIN

But my hopes were suddenly dashed when the water under the ice beneath my sledge began to roll and swell. The wind picked up, blowing hard and tossing me about as if I were in a tornado. Then, with a tremendous roar, the ice cracked apart, opening up deep, wide rifts like those in an earthquake.

Those rifts instantly filled with water, forming a turbulent sea. That sea now separated me, on a small piece of ice, from my evil enemy who floated away.

Soon, he had disappeared from sight, and I was left to die a hideous death. My sledge would be my coffin and a block of ice my burial place!

While I was on that ice—and I don't know how long it was—all my dogs, except one, died off. My food was gone, and I was about to sink when I saw your ship. I had no idea that any ships came this far north.

I broke apart my sledge to make oars, and managed to move the block of ice closer to your

An Evil Enemy Floats Away.

ship. And although I was weak and close to death, I had decided that if you were heading south, I wouldn't come aboard. I preferred taking my chances on surviving in the sea than let anything stop me from pursuing my enemy. But you were heading north, and so I let you rescue me.

You saved my life, you and your men, and although I'm still weak from my ordeal, I *do* plan to continue my pursuit. . . .

* * * * * *

Robert, my friend, that ends my story. I pray that I live long enough to find this terrible fiend and destroy him. But if I don't . . . if I die before I find him, you must promise to find him and take my revenge for me. Just remember, though, if he should appear before you, don't listen to anything he says. That fiend can be very persuasive. Don't trust him. Just kill him!

"I Let You Rescue Me."

"Are You Mad, Robert?"

CHAPTER 22

Peace at Last!

Victor Frankenstein's strange and terrifying story was at an end. Robert Walton sat back in awe. He felt great respect as well as great sympathy for this young scientific genius. Still, his curiosity was aroused.

"Victor," he asked, "now will you tell me how you formed this creature and how you brought him to life?"

"Are you mad, Robert? What do you want to do, create another fiend like this one? Do you have any idea what would happen if someone did that? If another monster were let loose to terrorize the world? . . . No, no one will ever know my horrible secret! It will die with me!"

Weeks went by with no change in the ice surrounding the ship. It still threatened to crush the small vessel to bits.

Victor grew weaker and weaker each day, and now couldn't even get out of bed to look for the sledge or to get some air on deck.

Then one day, a roar of thunder in the distance brought the entire crew out on deck. That roar signaled the cracking and splitting of the solid sea of ice. Two days after that, a path wide enough for the ship to sail through opened up. They were free!

When Captain Walton gave the order to lift anchor and set sail, a great shout went up from the crew. The overjoyed captain hurried down to the cabin to tell Victor that they were heading back to England at last.

"No, you can't go back," gasped Victor. "You must help me find my enemy first."

The Sea of Ice Cracks Open.

The captain shook his head sadly. "I can't expose my men to any more danger. Please try to understand that, Victor. I can't put my ambition for exploration or your desire for revenge above the safety of all these men."

"Then go if you must, but I can't go with you. My mission isn't over yet. I know I'm weak, but I have to go on." With that, Victor tried to lift his frail body out of bed, but the effort was too great. He fell back on the pillow in a faint.

When he regained consciousness, Victor had difficulty breathing and couldn't speak at all. The ship's doctor was called and after examining the gravely ill man, he gave the captain the sad news.

"He only has a few hours to live, sir. I'm sorry."

Robert sat by Victor's bed and stared, unmoving, at this man he had befriended.

After a while, Victor's eyelids fluttered, and he whispered, "Come closer, my friend, for I

"He Only Has a Few Hours to Live."

don't have much strength left. I know I'm dying, and I want you to know that my desire for revenge is gone.

"I realize now that *I* am to blame for deserting my creature after I formed him. I should have seen to it that he had a better life, with happiness and love. But it's too late for that now. Now, I have a responsibility to all mankind to see that this creature is stopped before he murders again. I can't do it myself any longer, and I beg you once again to do it for me."

With that, Victor grasped the hand of his last friend on earth. His lips spread in a soft, gentle smile and his eyes closed forever...

That night, as Robert was standing on deck thinking about his friend, he heard a hoarse voice coming from the cabin where Victor's body lay in its coffin.

Hurrying below deck, Robert flung open the door and found a gigantic creature bent over the coffin, weeping as he pressed Victor's cold,

A Gentle Smile and His Eyes Closed Forever.

stiff hand against the long, ragged hair hanging over his face. Unearthly groans seemed to come from his soul as he wept.

Seeing Robert at the doorway, the creature sprang towards the window.

"Wait! Stay!" called the captain.

The creature pointed down at Victor and said hoarsely, "He is my last victim. I only want him to pardon me now for destroying all the people he loved."

Robert's first impulse was to follow Victor's last wishes and kill the creature, but something in the creature's voice aroused the captain's pity and curiosity. "If you had asked for forgiveness sooner... if you had stopped your murderous acts of revenge sooner, Victor would still be alive. Do you understand? This is all your doing!"

"I hated what I was doing," replied the creature. "I was selfish and thought only of my own feelings, I admit it. But I wasn't always that way. I began life as a loving,

"I Want Him to Pardon Me Now."

sympathetic being. All I wanted was to have people ignore my ugliness and love me for the goodness inside me. But nobody did. Nobody gave me a chance. All anybody showed me was hatred . . . and that was only because of my ugliness. Even the man who created me felt that way. Yes, that's what changed me.

"Yet there was a time when I pitied Victor Frankenstein, seeing the misery I had caused him. But when I learned that he was planning to marry and have a happy life for himself, after taking away any chance of one for me, my pity turned to a thirst for revenge!"

Robert listened to the monster, first with pity, then with suspicion as Victor's warning echoed: *"He can be very persuasive."*

Then his suspicion turned to anger, and he shouted, "Evil wretch! First you drive him to his death, then you come here to ask his forgiveness. You don't know what it means to be sorry. The only thing you know is hate!"

"What do *you* know of hate? Why don't you

"I Will Burn My Miserable Body to Ashes."

hate Felix, who drove me from his cottage when I was just befriending his aged father? Why don't you hate the peasant who shot me after I saved his child from drowning? . . . I have been scorned and kicked and trampled. Isn't that reason enough to hate all mankind? You hate me too, Captain, . . . but not as much as I hate myself for murdering innocent and helpless people who never did me any harm.

"But don't be frightened. The only murder I plan to commit now is my own. I will leave your ship on the ice raft that brought me here and head north, to the coldest, most remote part of the globe.

"There, far away from the world, I will build a fire, my funeral pyre, and burn my miserable body to ashes. Then the wind will sweep those ashes into the sea, for I have no wish for any part of me to be found by a curious traveler who might attempt to create another being like me.

Planning His Own Murder

"And now I say, 'Farewell, world! . . . Farewell, Victor Frankenstein!'"

With those words, the creature leaped through the cabin window.

Robert sprang towards the window after him, but the creature was already on his ice raft, which lay close to the ship. As Robert watched, the raft was carried along by the waves.

In moments, the creature was far away, lost in the darkness . . .

"Farewell, World!"

Made in the USA
San Bernardino, CA
22 July 2019